Katie Fforde

Saving the Day

arrow books

1 3 5 7 9 10 8 6 4 2

Arrow Books
20 Vauxhall Bridge Road
London SW1V 2SA

Arrow Books is part of the Penguin Random House group
of companies whose addresses can be found at
global.penguinrandomhouse.com

First published in paperback by Arrow Books in 2021

www.penguin.co.uk

A CIP catalogue record for this book is available from
the British Library.

ISBN 9781787466241

Typeset in 12/16 pt ITC Stone Serif
by Integra Software Services Pvt. Ltd, Pondicherry

Printed and bound in Great Britain by Clays Ltd, Elcograf S.p.A.

The authorised representative in the EEA is Penguin Random House
Ireland, Morrison Chambers, 32 Nassau Street, Dublin D02 YH68.

Penguin Random House is committed to a
sustainable future for our business, our readers
and our planet. This book is made from Forest
Stewardship Council® certified paper.

TO THE WHOLE QUICK READS TEAM,

AND TO JOJO MOYES,

THANK YOU FOR YOUR DEDICATION IN
KEEPING THE SCHEME GOING.

Chapter One

Allie hung up her overall, pulled the tie off her hair and shook it loose, and then she picked up her bags of shopping. At last she could leave the supermarket where she worked and get into the September sunshine. Allie was tired and hungry and wanted a chocolate bar. She never seemed to see daylight when she was at work, and it got her down.

Once Allie was out of the building, she opened the multipack of Mars bars on the top of the bag and ate one as she walked. She finished at four on a Saturday, but the time always dragged.

Allie got on with most of the people she worked with, but there were two women, Edith and Rita, who always worked together and who really got her down. Edith and Rita were older than she was and always grumbling and telling Allie how to run her life. She was twenty but Edith and Rita made her feel younger. Allie thought it was partly because her mum lived in Canada, and had done since Allie was little. Edith and Rita seemed to think they had to take her mum's place.

One of the things Edith and Rita were always on about was why hadn't Allie and Ryan, her boyfriend, got married yet. Ryan was a lovely boy. They knew this because his mum, Dorothy, was their friend. Ryan was very good to his mum and thought the world of Allie, they told her. Edith, Rita and Dorothy were all married young, because they were pregnant, and Allie sometimes felt they wanted her to get married and have children so she would be the same.

Allie knew Ryan was good to his mum – she saw it. Besides, he had a bad tattoo on his arm of a heart with Mum written across it. He did her shopping, brought her flowers and often took her on outings. But Allie never felt that he thought the world of her, Allie. Ryan never took Allie anywhere except the pub, and then only if there was a match on, so he didn't have to talk to her. He never brought her flowers, or chocolates – or even a bar of chocolate. The most he could do was buy her a half of lager at the pub, and that was only when it was his round. Not for the first time, she thought about dumping Ryan, if only she could summon up the courage. They had been together since before they left school. They were together through habit.

As she passed Jango's café in the middle of the High Street, Allie slowed down. It was in a part of town that used to be a bit run down, but now new shops and businesses were starting up and there was a buzz about it. The café hadn't been there long and had an empty shop on one side of it. It was doing plenty of business, full of office workers, young mums with huge buggies and couples. In there, coffee was more than a teaspoon of Mellow Bird's in a mug. It was a treat – special.

Allie sighed. This was where she really wanted to work. In here the staff always seemed to be laughing and chatting with the customers. They wore bright aprons that looked attractive and fun. She loved the smell of coffee and cake that wafted out whenever anyone opened the door. There was one boy she quite fancied who always seemed to be laughing and joking with his colleagues. He was cute!

She stopped and looked in through the window. An older man, who she guessed was the owner, was cleaning the big coffee machine – it was nearly the end of the day. Several glass domes were arranged on the counter. When Allie passed on her way to work there were huge scones, muffins, giant biscuits and enormous layered sponge cakes inside them.

Now, there wasn't much left except the odd slice of cake, some crumbs and maybe a single scone. Once, when Allie had passed and the owner was cleaning up, she had seen him take the last piece of cake and a scone, wrap them up and then give them to a homeless person settled into a doorway nearby. Edith and Rita from the supermarket thought that homeless people were on the street because they didn't want to work – perhaps, Allie felt, because Edith and Rita had always worked so hard themselves. But Allie knew that sometimes bad things happened to people, and sometimes they ended up on the street. It wasn't always their fault.

Although Allie usually looked in the window, this time something was different. There was a card. *Kitchen assistant wanted. General help with some simple cooking.*

Her heart stopped. Her favourite place, the place where she wanted to work, was advertising. She couldn't believe it!

Allie didn't let herself think about it or she would never have dared – she just opened the door and went in.

'I'm here about the job,' she said, pointing at the notice.

The owner didn't speak right away, but then he nodded. He looked over at a younger man

4

who was stacking bottles in a fridge. It was the cute guy Allie liked. 'Si? You OK here?'

Si nodded. Allie glanced at him and noticed he looked even better in his tight T-shirt and apron than she had thought.

The owner smiled at Allie. 'I'm Mac and this is my café. Come into the office and have a chat.'

He showed her into a tiny office, just big enough for a desk and a couple of filing cabinets. 'Have a seat.'

Mac pulled out a stool from under a table.

Now she was here, Allie wanted to run out, to escape. Why had she thought she could work somewhere like this? She should stick to what she knew – stacking shelves at the supermarket.

'Why do you want to work here?' Mac asked.

Allie made herself think before she spoke. 'I've always wanted to work in a café like this.'

'Where do you work at the moment?'

'At the supermarket. I've worked there since I had a Saturday job and when I left school I just started working there full-time.'

'But you need a new challenge?' Mac smiled. He didn't seem to be judging her, which was nice. 'Are you interested in cooking?'

'Yes.' Allie shrugged. She liked watching cookery programmes on TV when she was alone in the house.

'I need someone who can knock up a batch of soup without too much trouble,' said Mac. 'Could you do that?'

'What, make soup?' asked Allie.

Mac nodded. 'Yep.'

Allie didn't know what to say. She didn't realise you could make soup. It was something that came in a tin or a packet. She shook her head.

'What about cakes?' Mac went on. 'Scones? Sandwiches?'

'I can make sandwiches,' she said. The sandwiches she made were thick, using sliced bread, but her dad often asked her to make them. 'And I do a wicked cooked breakfast.' Her dad loved her breakfasts with baked beans, fried bread and, sometimes, black pudding. 'I also do fried cheese sandwiches. My boyfriend likes them.'

'Let's go into the kitchen,' he said.

Allie looked around the kitchen with interest. It had stainless-steel worktops and a large mixer, like they had on *Bake Off*, only huge. There was a microwave – good to see some bit of equipment she knew how to work – and pots full of wooden spoons. There was a rack of knives on the wall. She spotted a potato masher, and something that could be used for bashing things, but really she didn't know what anything was. She felt down-hearted. She didn't really know very much about cooking, and didn't know how to use most of those gadgets.

'It's busy in here in the mornings,' said Mac. 'We're making scones, soup, salads, and quiches and pies. We bake our baguettes from frozen.' He grinned. 'It's mad but we love it. We have a good team. I just need another person to join us.'

Allie really wanted to work here. She knew the time would go quickly, that she would learn useful skills, meet new people, and she wanted to work for Mac. He didn't seem to be a bully like the few men she had worked with in the past. 'Could I have a trial?'

Mac breathed in deeply and then let go of his breath. 'To be honest, I want someone with a few more kitchen skills than you seem to have, but I like your attitude and in say ... a month, you could have a trial. A month would give you a chance to learn to cook one or two things. If you tried out now, you'd struggle. I don't want you to struggle – I want you to do well. I'd like you to work with us here.'

'But there won't still be a job in a month, will there?' said Allie. She knew she was sounding a bit desperate. 'You couldn't keep it open for me, not for a month.'

'True, but if you worked at learning what you need to know, I'd find space for you. Lots of us work part-time. Some would like more time off. I'd find some hours for you.'

Chapter Two

As she walked home Allie didn't know if she felt happy or let down. She didn't know enough about cooking for her dream job, but Mac, the man in charge, did want her to work there. He had given her time to learn to cook. But how would she learn those basic skills?

Her mother hadn't been around to teach her and even if she had, she wouldn't have known how to make soup. Her mother only really cared about her band and her music – she had a great voice – and had never been much of a home-maker. Although to be fair, Allie always knew her mother really loved her. She often sent letters and little presents, in between birthdays and Christmas, from her home in Canada.

She still hadn't decided if she was feeling happy or gloomy, when she noticed the woman next door's wheelie bin halfway down the road. It was annoying how the wheelie bins got blown about, if you didn't get them in as soon as they had been emptied. Allie went and fetched the bin. She didn't know the woman next door, she'd not long moved in, but she looked pleasant enough.

Allie was just putting the wheelie bin next to the shed by the front door when the woman came out. Mrs Ferris – that was her name, Allie remembered. Her dad had found it out.

'It's Allie, isn't it?' said Mrs Ferris. 'Thank you so much for saving my bin. Would you like a cup of tea as a reward?' Mrs Ferris smiled in a friendly way.

Allie suddenly did want a cup of tea. She'd have to make her dad one when she got home, but it would be good to have one herself first.

'And a biscuit,' said Mrs Ferris. 'I've just made them.'

'Oh. Yes, please!' said Allie. 'I'd love one!' And she followed Mrs Ferris into her house. Mrs Ferris had made the biscuits!

Once inside the house, Allie couldn't help staring. It had the same arrangement of rooms as their house, but was totally different. And it wasn't like an old lady's house, either. When her dad had told Allie they had a woman as their new neighbour, Allie had assumed he meant an elderly person. But Mrs Ferris wasn't that old. In fact, she was probably about the same age as Allie's mum.

There were ornaments, but not china ladies in old-fashioned dresses, or little boys, or cats, like Allie's gran had. Mrs Ferris had weird glass ornaments, and lamps made of pottery and wood.

There were pictures on the walls, shelves filled with books, photographs in frames in front of the books. And there were vases full of dried grasses, peacock feathers, chopsticks. Strange things – but Allie liked them.

'Go and sit down, then,' said Mrs Ferris. 'I'll bring the tea.'

Allie looked around as she waited. There was a fireplace with a gas fire and the shelf above held even more photographs.

Mrs Ferris came in with a tray. 'Can you take the papers off that table for me, please. Just put them on the floor.'

Allie did as she was asked. Mrs Ferris seemed to be doing a huge crossword puzzle.

'I like to do puzzles,' Mrs Ferris said. 'It's supposed to help your brain stay active.'

'My gran likes word searches.'

'There you go. Now, do you want sugar in your tea?'

'No thank you.' Her mother had once said sugar in your tea could make you fat. Allie thought about her mother every time someone asked if she wanted sugar in her tea.

'Right,' said Mrs Ferris. 'Try the biscuits. Chocolate chip. It's a new recipe.'

Mrs Ferris held out a plate of biscuits and Allie took one. Allie's gran would have given her a plate to put the biscuit on to stop crumbs going on the carpet. Mrs Ferris's carpet could have done with a quick hoover, Allie noticed. She bit into the biscuit and her eyes opened wide. It was amazing. It wasn't too sweet and the chocolate was yummy. It was crisp but crumbly.

'Did you really make these biscuits?' she asked.

Mrs Ferris smiled and nodded.

'They are insane! So good!'

'Have another,' said Mrs Ferris, holding out the plate.

Allie put out her hand, but then held back. 'Could I take one home for my dad?'

'Of course!' said Mrs Ferris, still smiling. 'I'll put some in a bag for you to take home. Have another one now.'

'How do you make biscuits like these?' asked Allie.

'Mostly you just mix flour, butter and sugar together and bake it.' Mrs Ferris looked at Allie a bit oddly. 'Have you never done baking? At school, maybe?'

Allie shook her head.

'Not with your mum either?'

Allie felt she had to explain about her mum. She didn't want Mrs Ferris to think badly of her. 'My mum was in a band. She sang and played the guitar and toured the country when I was little. She took me with her, of course, but I didn't like it so I came home to be with Dad. Then they got divorced and Mum married again.'

Allie paused. She had been teased at school because she didn't have a mum, although she wasn't the only one who didn't. 'Mum did ask me to go and live with her in Canada but who'd keep an eye on Dad if I wasn't here? Baking isn't really his thing.'

Allie laughed to think of her football-loving dad with a pinny on. He had kept her fed when she was a child though, and called himself the King of the Ready Meal. He never really did what Allie thought of as cooking. 'Although some men do baking. I love *Bake Off*.'

'Me too.'

'You could go on it!' said Allie. 'They always have an older lady on it.' She took a breath. 'Sorry, was that rude?'

'Not at all! I am an older lady. But I'm not good enough to go on *Bake Off*. My scones are good, my biscuits are OK and I can make a basic cake, but I can't do fancy icing.'

Allie had an idea and suddenly felt hopeful. 'Can you make other things?'

Mrs Ferris frowned. 'What sort of other things?'

'Soup?'

'Soup?' said Mrs Ferris. 'Yes, of course. When I was bringing up my family we ate a lot of soup.'

'Could you teach me how to make it?' asked Allie. Mrs Ferris could be the answer. If she could teach her how to cook, then Allie could go back to the café and possibly get a job there.

'Of course. It's not difficult. Why do you want to learn now?' asked Mrs Ferris. 'Are you trying to save a few pennies?'

'No! Do you know that café in the High Street – Jango's? They want someone to work in the kitchen. I've always wanted to work in a café like that, and there was a card in the window. The owner was really nice and said to come back when I had learned how to cook the basics. Soup was one of the things I need to make.' Allie realised all over again how much she wanted the job.

'I go into that café sometimes,' said Mrs Ferris. 'It's nice. And all the cakes are home-made. Not sure who makes them, but they're lovely.'

'It looks like a great place to work and I need a change,' said Allie.

'Well, that's a brilliant reason for wanting to learn to cook. When can you start your lessons?'

Allie pulled out her phone and checked the time. 'Not now. I'd better get back to Dad.'

'I'll put the biscuits in a bag for him.'

'It would be so kind of you to teach me to cook,' said Allie, when she was halfway out of the door.

'Wait until you've had a lesson before you thank me,' said Mrs Ferris. 'Are you working tomorrow?'

Allie shook her head. 'No.'

'Do you cook Sunday dinner for your dad?'

Allie shook her head again. 'Not from scratch. I buy everything frozen, and the chicken ready cooked.'

Mrs Ferris made a face and smiled. 'I'll teach you how to cook a proper roast another time. Can you call in tomorrow?'

Allie wasn't seeing Ryan that Sunday. He was taking his mother to a garden centre, and they would have Sunday lunch there. Then his mother would browse in the shop, which sold clothes and shoes, and they would go home. 'Yes. What time?'

'Eleven o'clock. We'll make soup for lunch. '

'That's very kind of you, Mrs Ferris.'

'See you tomorrow, dear. And you must call me Cherry.'

Allie felt it would be a while before she was able to do that.

*

'Dad?' Allie went into the living room. Her dad was there in his old reclining chair, watching football. He worked nights as a security guard so wouldn't have been up long.

'All right, Al?' her dad said. 'You're a bit late, aren't you?'

'Sorry,' said Allie. 'Were you worried?'

'Of course not,' her dad, Derek, said.

But Allie could tell he had been, a bit.

'I went to see about a new job. Then I went to see Mrs Ferris next door. She gave me a cup of tea and biscuits.' Allie shook the bag in her hand. 'She made them. She's going to teach me how to make them too. I'll put the kettle on.'

Chapter Three

'So, where were you last night?' said Ryan, scowling at Allie in a way that made her feel uneasy. He was quite a big lad, with a bit of a belly on him, and he could be a bit scary. It was just over a week since Allie had seen the job in the café advertised, and now Ryan was waiting for her by the door after work, so he could walk her home.

'I went round to see my neighbour. She's teaching me how to cook,' said Allie. She pulled up the hood on her parka. 'Let's go.' She was tired and wanted to go home.

'Why do you want to learn to cook?' said Ryan. 'You've managed fine up to now.'

Before Allie could answer, Edith butted in. Edith had been on the same shift as Allie and had come out at the same time as her, and now spoke for her.

'She wants a better job,' said Edith. 'She needs to cook fancy things for that.' Edith was a friend of Ryan's mum, and she thought Allie was lucky to be going out with Ryan. It seemed that Edith didn't want Allie to get a better job, either.

Allie had planned to tell Ryan about her wanting a new job when she had actually got it. She knew he wouldn't be keen on her cooking properly. He liked what she cooked now. She could do a cooked breakfast and make sandwiches. She could put oven chips in the oven, and if they bought a cooked chicken she could add some frozen roast potatoes to go with it. She could mix up gravy from granules.

Ryan thought that was all a girl needed to know. Ryan thought her job in a supermarket was all she needed, too. Allie didn't agree. Ryan hadn't had a job himself for a while. He never fancied anything suggested by the Job Centre and had managed to make them believe he had a bad back, so he got benefits.

'Don't be so silly,' said Ryan. 'You've got a job. You don't want another one. You wouldn't be able to handle it. You're not the sharpest knife in the box, are you?'

Ryan always made her feel she was stupid, although she knew she wasn't. It was just Ryan telling her she was thick, all the time. His father, before he left, had told Ryan that he was stupid, so it made him feel better to say the same thing to somebody else. Most of the time she didn't mind too much, but now it made her angry.

Allie thought about finishing with him right then and there. But she knew he would start shouting. Rita and Edith would join in the argument and, between them, they'd make Allie feel she was in the wrong. It was better to say nothing and carry on.

'Come on, let's go,' she said and set off walking. He caught her shoulder and pulled her back, and then started walking too. He didn't mind them leaving. He just didn't want her – Allie – deciding when. He was in a bad mood for some reason. He spent a lot of time playing games on his computer and sometimes they wound him up a bit.

Usually when Ryan was like this, Allie felt sick and wanted his mood to improve so he'd be nice to her. She felt he'd be happier if he found himself a job, but he'd got in an awful temper when she'd suggested it once. Besides, his mother liked having him at home most of the day. It was company for her.

He liked a cooked breakfast, thought Allie, whatever time of day it was. Perhaps she could make him one now. Although he didn't want her to learn to cook, he did like her being able to get his eggs just how he liked them. But Allie didn't feel like it now. She'd had enough of him. It was time for her to move on.

Because Ryan was with her, she didn't stop at the café and check if they were still looking for staff, although, out of the corner of her eye, she clocked the postcard. It was still there. That was good. Then she remembered Mrs Ferris next door was expecting her to call in. She was going to show Allie how to make American-style pancakes because her dad loved them. But Allie knew calling in to see Mrs Ferris would annoy Ryan. What should she do?

As they got nearer the house Allie said, 'I'm going to see Mrs Ferris for a moment. You go on. I won't be long.'

'But she's an old lady. What do you want to see her for?' Ryan was not happy.

'Look, you go and see Dad. Tell him I'll be along shortly. I've got the black pudding. I could make you both a full English for dinner if you like?'

'I'm coming in with you,' said Ryan. 'Make sure she doesn't keep you chatting.'

Allie sighed, but didn't say anything. She felt that Mrs Ferris could deal with Ryan if she had to. Plus, he'd see for himself that she wasn't that old.

'I'm afraid I can't come for my lesson today,' said Allie as soon as Mrs Ferris had opened the door.

'OK,' said Mrs Ferris. 'Is this Ryan? Hello, Ryan.'

Mrs Ferris looked at Ryan directly. She was smiling and friendly, but Allie knew Ryan wouldn't like her. He didn't answer Mrs Ferris. He just nodded.

'Would you like a cup of tea?' asked Mrs Ferris. 'I've made rock cakes.'

Ryan took hold of Allie's arm. 'Come on, Al!'

'I'll take that as a no, then,' said Mrs Ferris.

Allie couldn't look at her as she followed Ryan down the path. She felt really embarrassed by his rudeness. Mrs Ferris had been so kind to her, and had even made them a cottage pie which Dad had really liked. Even Dad liked Mrs Ferris now he'd got to know her a bit.

Just as she reached their front door she heard Mrs Ferris hiss. Allie looked back. Mrs Ferris winked. 'Come over tomorrow instead for your pancake lesson?'

Chapter Four

Ryan slept on the sofa that night. He'd got through quite a lot of lager last night and had fallen asleep in front of the telly. Allie was glad he had. She still slept in the narrow single bed she'd had since she was little, and it was very cramped for two. If Ryan shared it, she usually ended up on the floor when he turned over and pushed her out in his sleep. Now, when she came downstairs, she saw him snoring away, his feet on the arms of the sofa, the floor littered with empty beer cans.

It was still too early to go over to Mrs Ferris's, so she cleared up. She didn't actually run the hoover over the floor, although it badly needed it, but she didn't bother to be super-quiet.

When she was done, she made a mug of coffee, left it on the table near Ryan and said loudly, 'I'm going out now!'

Then she left, not bothering to find out if Ryan had heard her or not. She'd made him coffee – her duty was done. It wouldn't be how he saw it, of course, but she no longer cared.

The sun was shining, and she felt excited as she knocked on Mrs Ferris's door.

'Hello, love!' Mrs Ferris said. 'Come in. I'll just get some clothes on.'

Once she was in the kitchen, Allie saw the time. Nine in the morning! It was a bit early to call round, she realised, especially on a Sunday, but Mrs Ferris didn't seem annoyed. Allie tidied up her kitchen, and washed the couple of saucepans that were soaking. When Mrs Ferris came back the kitchen was spotless.

'Oh, Allie! You didn't need to do that! How kind of you. And you've done such a good job! Thank you,' said Mrs Ferris.

Allie wasn't used to being thanked. What she did at home or at work was taken for granted. Clearing up was what Allie did. She didn't expect to be thanked.

She felt herself get a little warm as Mrs Ferris looked at her, smiling, appreciating her work. She shrugged.

'Will you teach me to make pancakes, please, Mrs Ferris?' Allie said.

'Of course, if you try and call me Cherry.'

'Cherry,' said Allie, smiling.

'Well done! I used to be a teacher and I enjoy this,' said Cherry. 'Pass me my apron, please. It's on the back of the door. There's another you can use. Now, we need flour, a bit of baking powder ...'

'They're quite easy,' said Allie, a little later.

'They are,' Cherry agreed. 'And you make them very neatly. Now, let's eat some. I like them with butter and honey, but they're nice with fruit, too.'

They were delicious, eaten hot with the butter melting off them. 'And cheap as chips,' Cherry added.

Allie couldn't believe how good they were with so few ingredients. 'I'm going to write down all the recipes you've taught me.'

'Good idea. And you can add favourite recipes from other places – magazines, off the telly, things like that.'

When they'd eaten as many pancakes as they could, and Mrs Ferris had put the rest of them in the freezer, Allie said, 'I'd better go back. I told Dad I'd do a roast today. Well, what I call a roast!' Allie laughed, a bit ashamed by her shortcuts. 'I'll buy a cooked chicken and frozen roast potatoes and Yorkshire puddings. Gravy from granules ...'

'Frozen roast potatoes? Home-made are much nicer!' said Cherry.

'I'm sure they are, but I've never made them. Perhaps you could teach me next time?' Allie smiled, hoping Cherry wouldn't get fed up with teaching her how to cook things – even if she had been a teacher and said she liked it.

Cherry thought for a bit. 'Tell you what, why don't you and your dad come and have Sunday lunch with me? I haven't cooked a roast dinner for ages. It'll be fun. I've got a shoulder of lamb in the freezer. We can have that.'

Allie sighed. 'Ryan's at home,' she said. Ryan was there all the time now. Her dad was quite used to finding him there in the mornings.

'That's all right,' said Cherry. 'I'll make a crumble for pudding. I'll show you how to do that, too.'

'But Ryan was so rude before …'

'Yes, he was. But you go and ask your dad if he'd like to come and if he would, I'll do it. Ryan can please himself.'

Allie's dad was very happy at the thought of having a proper Sunday roast with Mrs Ferris. He had a shower and put on a clean shirt. Then he went out of the house and came back shortly afterwards with some flowers, a box of Roses chocolates and a bottle of wine. Allie realised he must like Mrs Ferris – Cherry – really quite a lot.

Ryan hardly spoke after Allie had said it was too late to make him a cooked breakfast and did he want a shower? She'd find him a towel. He said no to the shower. Allie realised that not working made him feel he didn't need to bother very much about being clean. It was one of those things she couldn't really talk to him about without him getting angry. When he'd first got laid off, she'd done her best to keep him feeling positive, but she'd realised he liked not working, and not washing that often.

Then he said, 'Make us a cup of coffee, Al.'

Allie handed him his can of Lynx at the same time as she gave him the coffee. She knew how he liked coffee, three sugars and lots of milk. He wasn't impressed by the Lynx.

'Are you saying I smell?' he asked, snatching the can out of her hand.

'No,' said Allie. But he did smell. And she thought the smell of Lynx was a bit better than the smell of Ryan unwashed.

'This is great, Cherry!' said Allie's dad when they were all sitting round the table that Cherry had put up in the living room. 'All home-made! Takes me back to when my mother used to do Sunday dinner.'

'Have some gravy, Derek,' said Cherry. 'Do you want some, Ryan?'

Ryan grabbed the jug and tipped the gravy on to his plate.

'Ryan!' said Allie. 'Leave some for the rest of us!'

'Stop nagging,' he said.

Allie was embarrassed and looked at Cherry, hoping she hadn't heard what Ryan had said.

'It's all right,' Cherry said calmly. 'I've got some more in the saucepan if we need it.'

After the crumble (which Cherry said was easy and that she would show Allie how to make another time), Ryan went home. He'd wanted Allie to go with him, but Allie said she had to wash up.

Derek sat on the sofa and looked around at the photos on the walls. He stopped at one of a young woman standing with a rock band. He peered at the photograph closely. 'Is that you with the Marshmallows? I loved them back in the day!'

'So did I!' said Cherry. 'I must have been their biggest fan!' she went on. 'That photograph is of my proudest moment, I think. I'd saved up all my money to get to the gig but, when I got there, all the cheaper seats had gone. They saw me outside the venue, looking as though the end of the world had come.'

'Didn't you get to see them, then?' Derek's concern was plain.

Cherry seemed a bit embarrassed. 'I did. They got me into the venue and then got their roadie to take the photo. It's my one brush with fame.'

'I like that. They were so good ...' Derek sighed.

'They still are good!' said Cherry. 'I've got their records, actual vinyl. Fancy a listen?'

'Yeah!'

Allie made them both a cup of tea and did the washing up. She didn't mind. She was thrilled to see her dad so happy, listening to the Marshmallows, chatting away. She knew he'd been lonely since her mum had finally left home for good. He'd had a few girlfriends, of course. But none of them had wanted to take on a man with a small daughter to look after. Deep down she felt it was her fault her dad was still on his own.

When she'd finished and had thanked Cherry for the lunch, Allie went home. She left her dad on the sofa, laughing with Cherry as if they were old friends. Allie was delighted.

Chapter Five

'You took your time,' said Ryan.

'I helped clear up,' said Allie crossly. It wasn't like he would ever offer to wash up or anything.

'You shouldn't have. Silly old cow.'

'Dad's still there. And she's not old and she's certainly not silly. You ate enough of her food!'

Ryan shrugged. 'I was hungry. You wouldn't cook me breakfast!'

'This isn't a hotel, Ryan!' Allie was angry. 'Cherry was very kind to ask us round for Sunday dinner.'

But Ryan had already switched on the telly and was flicking through the channels looking for a boxing match. He always had to have some sort of entertainment – he could never just talk to her. 'Make me a coffee, love,' he said, staring at the screen.

Allie went into the kitchen. Tomorrow she would ask at the café again, to see if she'd learned enough about cooking to work there now. And then she'd finish with Ryan. She put the kettle on. He wouldn't like her ending it between them. He'd want to be the one to do that. But if she wanted to change her life, she was the one who had to do it.

She gave Ryan his coffee, hoping it was the last drink she ever made for him.

'You know I don't like boxing,' she said, 'so I'm going out for a bit.'

'Allie!' he snapped. 'You can't do that! Come and sit down!'

'If you try to stop me, you'll miss the boxing.' She knew his mother was out for the day and he didn't want to go home. He'd rather stay here and be waited on.

She went upstairs and found an old exercise book from school. She'd only used a few pages, so it would be perfect for her to write recipes in. She tore out the used pages and went downstairs. She didn't want to go out, but if she stayed in, Ryan would want her to do things for him. And she wasn't doing that any more.

She walked to the corner shop, and bought some biscuits that her dad liked before going round to the little park. She hoped the boxing match would be over by the time she got back, and that Ryan would have got fed up and gone home. She really didn't want to see him.

She was lucky. The house was empty when she got back. Her dad must still be listening to old records at Cherry's. When she'd made herself a cup of tea, she cleared a space on the table and started writing out the recipes she'd learned from Cherry. She had a good memory, but she wanted them written down. Those recipes were her future. They'd get her out of the supermarket and, with luck, into a job she'd love.

She was still feeling strong in the morning when she set off to work, and she repeated her decision as she walked along. If she got the job she'd get rid of Ryan. She knew she'd find it harder to dump him if she still worked at the supermarket, where Rita and Edith thought the sun shone out of him. She thought about Cherry, too. She'd started out as Mrs Ferris, the new neighbour. Now it felt as if this kind lady had changed Allie's life. And maybe – just maybe – she was changing Allie's dad's life, too.

Chapter Six

Edith and Rita were on the same shift as Allie again. And they were even more annoying than usual that day. They'd heard about everyone going to Cherry's house for Sunday dinner.

'Ryan said that woman who lives next door to you is odd,' said Rita. 'He doesn't like you spending time there.'

Allie wasn't going to put up with this. 'Ryan liked her food well enough! He should be glad Cherry is teaching me to cook!'

When she left at the end of her shift, she was more determined than ever to get a new job at the café. She checked there was still a card in the window asking for workers and looked through the window to make sure that Mac, the boss, was in. There he was, sharing a joke with Si, the fit boy Allie liked. She reminded herself she must focus on her job, not a boy. She opened the door and went in.

It was only as she walked from the door to the counter that she remembered the recipes that she had written down so carefully. She should have brought the notebook with her to give her confidence.

'Hello!' she said bravely. 'Do you still need people to work here?'

Mac looked at her and smiled. 'It's you! You've come back! Have you learned to cook?'

'Yes!' said Allie. 'Well, some things.'

'What can you make, then?' Mac asked.

'Soup and cheese scones.' These were the things she knew she could remember how to make because the ingredients didn't have to be the same every time but could be adapted a bit.

'Sounds good. Maybe you'd better come into the kitchen and show me.'

Allie was nervous about going back into the kitchen, but she thought of her current job and Ryan. If she got this job she'd get rid of both – for ever. That was worth being a bit brave for.

'Soup takes a bit of time to cook,' said Mac. 'So maybe you could make a batch of cheese scones?'

Allie took a deep breath. She hadn't expected to make scones before she'd even got the job. But she couldn't back out now. 'OK.'

'There's the basin to wash your hands in and I'll find you an apron. Ask me for what you need and get going.'

'I'll need self-raising flour, some eggs, some butter, cheese, cayenne pepper, and have you got any yoghurt?'

'Whoa!' said Mac. 'Slow down, girl! That's a lot of things to remember. Si? Can you find us the self-raising flour? Cayenne pepper is in the storeroom. I'll fetch it. I won't be a tick. And yes, we do have yoghurt. It's in the fridge with the butter, cheese and eggs.'

Mac showed Allie the big walk-in fridges that were in a storeroom at the back of the kitchen, in case she needed more of anything. Then he said, 'I have to pop out for a minute now. I'll be back in time to taste the scones. We've got Jessie out front, and Si will sort you out here if you need any help, won't you, Si?'

'Sure will!' said Si. 'It'll be a pleasure.'

Allie felt his eyes on her and she glanced at him. There was something about the way he looked at her that made her blush. She hoped Si would think it was because it was quite warm in the kitchen. She would hate to think he had guessed that she liked him.

'Shall I turn the oven on for you?' said Si as he plonked a container of flour down on the bench in front of her. 'What temperature would you like?' He smiled and, not only did he seem really

34

helpful and friendly, he was even more attractive close up. He smelt nice – some aftershave that wasn't Lynx.

'Quite hot. My neighbour and friend who taught me to make these scones had a gas oven. She put it at number eight.'

'We have a gas oven too. Number eight it is,' said Si.

Si seemed to really want Allie to do well, and for her scones to turn out beautifully. He stood at her side, watching closely, in case she needed anything.

The part of making the scones that really worried her was the cayenne. It was very strong and too much could make the scones too fiery for most people.

'I'm not sure how much to put in,' Allie said to Si.

'Well, you've got quite a bit of flour there,' said Si. 'I reckon you'd be safe with half a teaspoon. If it's a bit too little, put in more next time!'

Allie smiled at him. He was so different to Ryan, who was always on her case, nagging her, wanting things from her, waiting for her to make him cross.

'We can use the machine to grate the cheese,' he said, when he saw she'd got out the cheese. 'I'll show you how to work it.'

Later he found the pastry brush when she said she was going to put long gratings of cheese on top of the scones. He gave her a double high-five when the scones were finally in the oven.

'How long do they take to cook?' Si asked.

'Between ten and fifteen minutes,' said Allie. 'I've made them quite large, so probably it'll be fifteen.'

Jessie, who'd come into the kitchen to fetch something, said, 'I can't wait to try them. They smell amazing. I think they'd sell well. Not everyone likes sweet things.'

The moment came. Fifteen minutes later, the kitchen timer went off. Allie opened the double doors of the oven. Her tray of scones was alone on the top shelf. Her hands protected with oven gloves, she pulled out the tray and put it on the stainless-steel work surface. She took off the gloves and picked up a scone. They looked beautifully golden brown on top, but she remembered Mrs Ferris – Cherry – telling her to check the bottom to make sure that was also brown.

'I think they're done,' she said, nervously, almost wishing she could put them back into the oven where no one could eat them.

Mac, the owner, had come back from his errand. Si and Jessie were also there. They all wanted to taste the scones.

'I've got some butter here,' said Jessie.

'They're better with butter,' said Allie. She didn't like everyone looking at her, or being the centre of attention. She liked to be at the back, more or less out of sight.

Mac cut open a scone and put a big slab of butter on to one of the halves. He took a big bite. 'That is amazing!' he said after a moment.

Everyone else took a bit of scone and put butter on it. They all said the same thing in different words. They loved the scones.

'I don't care if you can't make soup or anything else,' said Mac. 'Come and work for me and keep making those scones! Cheese scones are going on the menu now!'

Mac told Allie to take home a couple of the scones, so she could show Cherry how well they'd turned out. She'd told him how Cherry had helped her and he seemed pleased. 'It was a good call asking your neighbour to teach you to cook. Sharing skills is a good thing.'

It was agreed that she should start at the café as soon as she'd worked out her notice at the supermarket. Allie had some holiday owing to her, so she hoped to be in the café on the next Monday. But before that, she had to get rid of Ryan.

Chapter Seven

Ryan was her first proper boyfriend and Allie didn't know how to dump him. She was pretty sure he wouldn't mind not having her in his life. But she knew his pride would be hurt. She had to do it as kindly as possible. Which meant she couldn't just send a text. She worked all this out as she walked back from the café, but thought she might ask Cherry about it when she gave her the scone she had with her.

Cherry was thrilled with the scone. 'This is better than the ones I make!' she said. 'You're a natural. You have a light hand. I'm proud of you!'

'I wrote down the recipe as I made them,' said Allie, pleased but also embarrassed by the compliment. 'In case I was asked to make them again, and so other people could make them if the customers liked them.'

'How sensible of you!' said Cherry. 'When I'm cooking I always just guess and hope it turns out all right.' She chuckled.

'I think that's fine if it's just at home,' said Allie. 'But I think it's different for a café.'

'You're right – it is. And I'm thrilled they worked out so well and you've got the job.' Cherry paused. 'Now, what about Ryan? Are you going to finish with him?'

Allie nodded. 'I thought I'd ask him out for a drink tonight and tell him then. I don't want to put it off. There's a football match at the pub, so he should be all right about going there.'

'Won't he suspect something's up when you ask to meet him there? Don't you usually just see each other at home?' Cherry asked.

'I expect he will know something's up, but I can't think of another way. It would be wrong to just send him a text,' said Allie.

'How would Ryan dump you?' ask Cherry.

'He'd ghost me,' said Allie.

'Sorry, but what does that mean?'

Allie laughed. 'It means he'd block my number on his phone, and never get in touch again.'

'You don't want to do that to him?'

Allie shook her head. 'It's wrong. We've been going out for a long time even if he hasn't really got feelings for me any more. I have to tell him face-to-face. Besides, he'd just come round to my house. I don't think I could stop him doing that.' She felt a flash of fear. She certainly couldn't stop him doing that even if she didn't dump him by text.

'Maybe you dumping him will give him a push into getting a job,' Cherry said.

'Maybe.' But Allie was doubtful. Ryan liked living with his mum, with enough money from his benefits to go the pub sometimes and buy a few video games. Work would take some effort, and Ryan didn't like that.

'We'll have a cup of tea when you've arranged to meet Ryan. And is your dad at home? You could ask him if he'd like to join us. He could eat the scone you brought him in company.'

'Oh, OK.'

Allie sent a text to Ryan saying: *Meet me at the Fox at six. I've got something I want to say.* When it had sent, she said, 'He'll know I'm dumping him. He won't be happy. He likes things to stay the same.'

'Is he very fond of you?' Cherry looked as if she'd be surprised if he was.

'No. He won't miss me as a person,' said Allie. 'But he won't like being dumped. I'll go and see if Dad is up for tea and a scone at yours.'

Derek was up for it, but he insisted on changing into a clean shirt and some jeans instead of baggy joggers. He had a good wash first, too.

Allie could tell he really liked Cherry and she hoped Cherry liked him. But she couldn't tell for sure, as Cherry was friendly and welcoming to everyone. And while she really wanted him to have someone nice in his life, she did worry about what would happen to her. A job at the café would never pay enough for her to rent a flat on her own.

Allie was nervous walking to the pub to meet Ryan. She arrived first and ordered a pint of Ryan's favourite lager. She had half a shandy herself. She was more nervous than she had been when she went into the café to ask for a job. Although that had been more important, she knew that there would not have been any raised voices or trouble even if she had been turned down. Now things were bound to turn nasty.

Ryan was half an hour late. Allie sat sipping her shandy and looking at Ryan's pint, hoping he'd turn up soon. She wasn't surprised he was late – he always went at his own speed and didn't bother with anyone else. But, as the football match was due to start fairly soon and he liked to be there from the beginning, it wouldn't be long now.

Ryan looked angry the moment he appeared in the pub doorway, looking round for her. That was partly why she'd ordered the pint, so he'd see it at the same time as he saw her. He strode over to Allie's table, picked up the lager and drank nearly half of it. Then he sat down.

'So, what's this about then?' he growled.

Allie took a breath and tried to keep calm. She hoped her voice wouldn't shake when she spoke. 'I don't want to go out with you any more, Ryan,' she said. Her plan had been to leave the pub as soon as she'd told him, but he was sitting on a chair that blocked her exit.

'Got someone else, have you?' He drank some more lager.

'No. It's just not working for me any more,' Allie said, wondering how on earth she could escape. Her back was against the wall and Ryan was sitting right in front of her.

'"Not working for you any more," is it?' Ryan put on a high, childish voice. 'So, you think I care, do you?'

'No—'

'Well, let me tell you one thing, sweetheart!' He put his face very close to Allie's and she leaned back as far as she could – but a bit of spit still landed on her cheek. 'You don't finish with me, girl. I finish with you. OK? And I'm telling you now, no one is going to want to go out with you, so you'd better get used to the idea of being single!'

'OK, Ryan, whatever you like.' She stood up, stepped on her chair, put her foot on the table, jumped across it and down the other side. She was out of the pub before Ryan had finished saying 'Hey, you!'

She felt oddly lonely as she walked home. She didn't like Ryan and he didn't like her. But they'd been a couple for a long time, so it was odd knowing she was single.

She decided she wouldn't tell Edith and Rita at work that she and Ryan had split up. They'd find out anyway when Ryan told his mum, and they'd make such a big deal of it and act like Allie and Ryan were getting divorced or something.

Sadly, it didn't take long for the news to get back to her workmates. She handed in her notice and, by the next day, feedback from Ryan came through.

'You're mad leaving a good solid job like this one to work in that café,' said Rita. 'No wonder Ryan's not happy about it and dumped you.'

Allie shrugged. If that's how Ryan wanted to play it, it was fine by her. She hadn't told Ryan about her new job, but he obviously knew now.

'You should have hung on to him. You need to know how to keep a man,' said Rita, who, Allie knew, had had several relationships.

Allie shrugged again. 'Maybe we weren't right for each other.'

'That's soppy nonsense – "being right for each other",' said Edith. 'You get a man, you're nice to him, do what he wants, and he stays with you.'

'So, what went wrong for you, Edith?' said Allie. She knew she was stupid to answer the woman, but she couldn't help it.

Edith tossed her head. 'Ryan's better off without you!'

'I'm sure he is,' said Allie.

'But don't think he'll walk away and not do anything,' put in Rita. 'He'll get you back.'

Chapter Eight

Allie was very on edge walking to the café on her first morning at work. She was to start at eight thirty in the morning. The previous evening, Cherry had taught her to make special choux pastry so she could make éclairs. Neither Allie nor Cherry thought the café sold éclairs, but they both agreed Allie should know how to make them – just in case.

She had the recipe written in her book, and she had the book in her backpack. She also had white trainers and a clean T-shirt to wear with her jeans. She knew they'd give her an apron to put on top of her own clothes, but didn't know what else to expect.

As she got nearer Jango's she could hear the homeless guy, who was Scottish, playing his penny whistle. She knew him by sight because she used to pass him on her way home from the supermarket, and she always put some money in his hat. She liked the tune he was playing and he gave her a cheeky grin as she passed him, and she smiled back. It felt as if she had a friend nearby.

Mac opened the door to her when she arrived. 'Come on in. Have a brew before we start work. I've got the fruit scones on and maybe you'd like to do your party piece and make cheese ones?'

'I hope they go as well as the batch I made the other day!' said Allie. She was feeling a bit more confident as Mac was so friendly.

'I'm sure they will. Look, mine are ready now. We'll have a scone with our tea – breakfast – and then you get cracking on the cheese ones. When they're in the oven I'll show you the till, and teach you other things you need to know.'

Jessie came in soon afterwards and switched on the big coffee machine. 'This is the beast,' she said. 'It makes a lot of noise but if you're careful, it'll make wonderful coffee that people love. Ever made a cappuccino before?'

'Never. I'm not even sure what a cappuccino is!' said Allie. She'd feel better if she'd ever drunk a cappuccino, but she hadn't.

'It's all about the milk,' said Jessie. 'Most coffees have two shots of coffee, but it's the amount of milk that makes them different from each other. But we'll go through all that. I'll have you drawing hearts in the foam before you know it. It's fun!' Jessie patted her on the shoulder. 'You're going to be good at this. I can tell.'

Allie didn't feel she was good it. Jessie got her to practise using takeaway cups, and Mac took the wonky frothy coffees to the homeless guy, Jock, and his friend, Pete, round the corner. They got bacon sandwiches as well.

'We're all only a couple of steps away from homelessness,' Mac said, as he set off with his packages. 'So I give them what I can. They like coffee and bacon butties in the morning.'

'They move somewhere else when they've had breakfast,' Jessie told Allie. 'They know it's bad for business if they're hanging around. But they come back when it's quiet after lunch and see if there's anything left over. Mac's a kind man. They respect him for that.'

It was hard trying to remember everything, Allie thought. But she was doing fine until the customers began to come into the café more quickly later in the morning. So far, she'd avoided serving anyone. She'd cleared tables, stacked the dishwasher and fetched things, but she hadn't actually made anyone a cup of coffee.

'OK, Allie!' said Jessie. 'You serve these customers. Big smile first and then "Can I help?" Or "What can I get you?"'

Allie felt shy. At the supermarket she had spent most of her time stacking shelves because no one else liked it. She hadn't worked on the checkout that often. But she'd wanted to work in a café, and that meant talking to the customers, so she'd better get on with it!

'What can I get you?' she asked the young woman who was standing in front of the counter, tapping the top with her credit card. She looked like she was in a hurry.

'My usual please,' she said. Then the woman realised she hadn't seen Allie before. 'You're new!'

Allie smiled. 'It's my first day.'

'First days at work are hard!' said the young woman. 'Well, what I like is ...'

Allie at last managed to give the woman what she asked for and she went away, holding her coffee, happy, calling out a cheery 'Thank you!'

'There,' said Jessie. 'You've served our most tricky customer. She's nice, but she's very picky about her coffee. But she went out happy though, so that's a result!'

'I never thought I'd get it how she likes it,' said Allie. 'Just the right amount of milk and froth and chocolate sprinkles.'

'You've done the hardest bit. Now it's time to get ready for the lunchtime rush.'

*

Allie was standing in the storeroom looking about her in despair, certain she'd looked at every box in there, when Si came in.

'Can I help?' he said.

'Napkins,' she said. 'We're completely out. Jessie asked me to get some and they must be in here somewhere.' She wiped her damp hands on her apron.

'Napkins, for some reason, are kept here.' Si moved two boxes of fruit tea bags and uncovered a huge plastic-covered pack of napkins. 'Here, let me open them. They're hard to get out if you haven't got something to rip the plastic with.'

Si pulled a bottle opener with a hook on the end from his pocket and slashed through the plastic. 'Here.' He handed her several smaller packs of napkins. 'This should keep you going for a while.'

'Thank you so much! I've just got to fill the dispensers on the tables with them now.'

'You're doing really well, Allie,' said Si gently. 'You're having a brilliant first day!'

Allie gave him a shy smile before going back into the café with an armful of napkins.

At the end of her shift, Allie thought she'd never get the hang of her new job. Her feet were killing her, and it was such hard work with so many different things to learn. Si was going home at the same time as she was and offered to give Allie a lift to the end of her road.

'I remember how tough my first day was,' Si said as they drove. 'I thought I'd made a big mistake swapping a desk job for one where you never sat down!'

'Why did you give up the desk job?' Allie asked. She felt shy, but Si was so friendly that she felt it was all right to ask him.

'It was boring! No two days are the same in the café. I like the flexible hours, too. It gives me time to work on my own stuff. And Mac is great to work for. He has high standards but he backs his workers.' He grinned at her quickly.

'He took a big chance when he took me on,' said Allie. 'I've never worked in a café before.'

'But you made great cheese scones!' said Si. 'Are you working tomorrow?'

'Yes. Mac said it would be best if I kept going so I wouldn't forget everything.'

'That's good! I'm on tomorrow too. I'll keep an eye out for you. It's easy when you know everything, but the learning part is hard.'

Allie cleared her throat. 'So, what do you do when you're not working at the café? Do you mind me asking?'

He laughed. 'Not at all! I make music, but I do it with electronic stuff.' He paused. 'Shall I drop you here?'

'Yes, please,' said Allie. 'And thank you very much for the lift.'

'You're welcome! See you tomorrow.'

They smiled at each other. 'See you tomorrow,' she echoed and got out of the car.

Over the next two days or so, Allie's confidence grew. The customers liked her cheese scones so much that they were even called 'Allie's Cheese Scones' on the chalkboard, and people came in and asked for them. Her cappuccinos were improving too. She could do a bit of a swirl in the foam and was working on a heart pattern.

'That's for boys you fancy,' said Jessie. 'You put a heart on their coffee and they know.'

Allie laughed. She couldn't imagine ever being bold enough to try and pick up a customer! Anyway, she still fancied Si, who was really helpful, but so far had shown no interest in her beyond being a really good friend. Maybe she should make him a cup of coffee and put a heart on it!

Chapter Nine

On the Friday, when Allie was nearing the end of her shift in the café and looking forward to a weekend of doing nothing except watch telly, Ryan came in. He had been drinking, and although Allie's heart sank when she saw him, she wasn't really surprised. She'd suspected he wouldn't just leave her alone after she'd dumped him. And now here he was, and he was holding a baseball bat.

If Allie had been behind the counter, as usual, she could have called for Si to come and support her. But as it was, she was clearing the counter from the front, putting all the cakes and scones that had been there all day into a box. Mac would take them to the homeless crowd later. There was no barrier between her and Ryan. She swallowed, trying not to show she was frightened.

'So, you thought you were better than the rest of us, getting a job in a fancy coffee shop!' Ryan said. He was banging his hand with the baseball bat, looking round the café for something to break.

Allie had thought he was going to hit her with the bat, but when she realised he meant to break up the café, it felt worse.

'Ryan, put the bat down,' she said, raising her voice, hoping Si would hear and come out and help her. 'If you do any damage, you'll get yourself into serious trouble!'

'You sound like a teacher who can't control her class,' said Ryan.

Allie knew he was right, so she made her voice stronger. 'You're just one person, Ryan, and I'm telling you to put the bat down!'

She was about to call out to Si when she remembered he was in the walk-in fridge, doing a stock check. This was a job that was done at the end of the day when the café wasn't busy. He wouldn't hear her, however loudly she called.

Ryan seemed to be enjoying himself. He looked around the café and found a packet of biscuits on a shelf. He picked it up and threw it at a row of soft-drink bottles. One of them fell, knocking down more packets and ending up on the floor. Luckily it didn't break. Ryan was obviously disappointed. He picked up the glass bottle and smashed it on the floor.

Then he got another packet of biscuits and threw that at the row of bottles, as if he were playing skittles. He threw harder and this time the bottle did shatter as it landed.

'Ryan!' said Allie as firmly and loudly as she could. 'Stop! Get out of here!'

'Why? I'm having fun!' He took a packet of tea and hit it with the bat as if it were a ball.

'Ryan!' Allie was so angry she forgot to be frightened. How dare he come in here and break up the café? 'Leave this café immediately!'

'Or what?' said Ryan. He batted another packet of tea into the corner, dislodging some boxes of macaroons.

'I'm going to make you!' Fury made her feel strong, although her brain told her she wasn't stronger than Ryan.

'You and whose army?' said Ryan.

'My army!' came a voice. It was Jock, his Scottish accent making him sound really tough.

Allie had been looking at Ryan so hard that she hadn't noticed anyone come into the café. They had come in quietly, not wanting Ryan to hear them. She turned round and saw that Jock had his friend, Pete, with him. They were looking at Ryan. They looked as if they were ready for a fight.

'And who are you?' said Ryan. Allie could tell he was rattled. He was big, but he wasn't fit and wouldn't fancy his chances against *two* men.

'We're people who happen to like this coffee shop as it is,' said Jock. 'With no broken bottles, no broken biscuits, and no young women being bullied. We suggest you take yourself out of here, pal, before your face bumps into my fist!'

Ryan tried to leave, but neither of the men in front of him moved. Jock hadn't finished.

'And if you ever threaten this café, or anyone who works here, anywhere, and at any time, we will find out and come after you!' Jock looked as if he meant every word he said.

The men stepped aside and Ryan went to the door. Everyone watched him start to run as soon as he was clear of the café.

Allie found she was shaking now the danger was past. 'Thank you so much, guys!' she said. 'He's my ex and can be nasty. Who knows how much damage he'd have done if you hadn't turned up!'

'We worked out something was wrong when we saw him coming in here with a baseball bat in his hands,' said Jock. 'He walked past us, stinking like a brewery. When we saw him come in here, we followed.'

'I'll make you both a drink,' said Allie, knowing it was what Mac would want her to do. 'What would you like? Tea or coffee? I'm quite good at doing cappuccinos now!' It wasn't long ago that these men had drunk her first attempts to put froth on top of a coffee. She felt so grateful to them.

They asked for tea and Si arrived behind the counter just as Allie had got them both seated.

'What's been going on?' Si asked. 'Are you OK, Allie? What have I missed?'

'My ex came in,' said Allie. 'I thought he was going to wreck the place, but these guys were heroes and stopped him. What cakes can we give them as a reward? I'll make brownies at home later, but they deserve something now.'

Si took a plate and started filling it.

Soon Mac came in and he had to be told the story too, although he didn't seem to have his whole mind on what Allie was saying.

'Thank you so much, lads! And Si? I know you're due to work for another couple of hours both of you, but why don't you give Allie a lift home? She's had a scary time of it.'

As Allie changed into her old trainers and took off her apron, she realised that, although Mac was pleased with how things had turned out, he wasn't totally happy.

'Do you think something's up with Mac?' she asked Si as she got into his car.

Si nodded. 'I know he was going to a business meeting with the landlord. Perhaps they're going to put the rent up. It's only a small café. Mac may not be able to afford more rent.'

'Oh no!' said Allie. 'It would be awful if the café closed down.'

Si sighed. 'I'd hate it too,' he said. 'We all love Jango's and I would hate to work anywhere else.'

Allie wouldn't want to work anywhere else either – not now, when she loved her job so much and felt so lucky to have got it.

Chapter Ten

Allie walked down the path to Cherry's house thinking about Si. She knew it was selfish, but if the café closed, she wouldn't see him any more. That was another reason for her to dread it closing. It was unlikely they'd both get jobs in the same place again. They got on so well and she really liked him. Maybe, given a bit more time, he would see her as someone to go out with, not just someone to help out at work.

Soon, Allie was sitting at Cherry's kitchen table in front of a cup of tea and a piece of cake. She told Cherry how Jock and his friend had come in and saved her from a furious Ryan.

Cherry was delighted. 'I know those lads. The Scottish one plays the penny whistle? I think he's good! And you see, all those snacks and cups of coffee Mac has given them in the past made them look out for you and the café when it was needed. Do you feel safe from Ryan now?'

'I do,' said Allie. 'But we think Mac's worried about the café. Si said he'd been to a meeting with the landlord. I really hope Jango's won't close down.'

'That would be such a shame,' said Cherry. 'Do you think it might?'

'If the rent goes up and Mac can't pay it, it might. We're very busy but quite small. Maybe we're too small to pay more rent?'

'I hope not. You've done so well getting a job there and making a success of it,' said Cherry.

Allie was still embarrassed by people praising her. She looked around her to find something else to talk about. 'You've put up new shelves. They look great.'

'Your dad put them up for me,' Cherry said. 'I needed them for my collection of jugs. I haven't unpacked them yet.'

'Oh! That's nice,' said Allie. 'I'm glad Dad was useful.'

'You don't mind?' asked Cherry.

'No. Why would I mind if you have new shelves?'

Cherry laughed. 'I didn't really mean did you mind about the shelves. I meant, did you mind that Derek put them up for me?'

Allie thought this was an odd question. 'My dad can do what he likes!' Then she realised what Cherry meant. 'Are you telling me that you and Dad have something going on between you?'

'A little bit, yes.' Cherry looked embarrassed.

'I think that's lovely!' said Allie. 'He's been lonely since Mum left.' She paused. 'I did think he looked a bit smarter and now I know why!'

'Well, I'm very glad,' said Cherry. 'We were worried it might bother you. You and me are such good friends now – I would hate it if anything spoiled that. I'll tell your dad you're fine with it. He'll be delighted.'

'Good,' said Allie.

'So, what about *your* love life? Has Si asked you out yet?'

Allie had told Cherry how much she liked Si one evening when Cherry had been teaching her to make pastry, and had opened a bottle of wine. 'I think he sees me as a new fellow-worker he needs to keep an eye on, not someone to ask out. I mean, he's really friendly and everything, but that's it.'

'That's a shame,' said Cherry. 'But give it time.'

'That's all I can do. I'm not going to ask him out first! He might laugh at me.' She thought about it. Si wouldn't laugh. He was far too kind for that. 'Or he might say something like "You're sweet but I'm in a relationship", which would be awful.'

'Maybe that's it,' Cherry agreed. 'If he's already going out with someone else, it would be wrong to ask you out.'

'That's true! I don't know if it's good that he doesn't play around when he's with someone, or bad because it means he'll never be mine!'

'Never say never!' Cherry patted Allie's hand.

Allie made a face and bit her lip. 'I'd better go home. If Dad's there, I'll tell him what great shelves he's put up for you, and then watch him go red in the face!'

'Horrid girl!' said Cherry brightly. 'I'm cooking dinner later. I'm expecting you and your dad to come.'

Mac seemed his usual cheerful self when Allie went to work the next morning, so she stopped being worried about Jango's and whether it might close. Si seemed a bit more friendly, too. At times she caught him looking at her and then looking away quickly, almost as if he fancied her. The days went by, and she became more and more relaxed as she found she was getting really good at her job.

She was very happy about her dad and Cherry becoming more than just friends, too. Her dad was so much more cheerful and easy to be around now, as well as being much more helpful in the house. Allie wondered what would happen to her if Cherry and Derek wanted to move in together, but decided not to worry about that until it happened.

Then, one day, at the café, Mac got everyone together in the kitchen.

'Bad news, I'm afraid, guys,' he said. 'The rent's going up and I can't pay it. We do fine as we are now, but with an increase in rent, I just can't make a profit. I can't make enough to pay the wages.'

Allie felt sick.

'We've got another two months, but then we're closing,' said Mac. 'I'd like to keep going until then, and not look as if we're dying on our feet. But if any of you feel you have to leave now and look for other work, I will understand.'

Allie wanted to cry, but didn't want to show herself up in front of everyone. She bit her lip.

'I'll stay till the end,' Si said at once. He was clearly supporting Mac as much as he could.

'So will I!' Allie said, her voice a bit croaky. It wasn't only that her dream job was coming to an end – it was that the café was a great place that people loved. It was tragic that it had to close.

Chapter Eleven

Allie was keen to make her last weeks at the café as good as they could be. She asked Mac if she could add home-made brownies to the menu. He'd tasted one of the ones she'd made for Jock and Pete, and he said yes, definitely. More and more of what they sold was being made in the café.

'Makes it cheaper,' said Mac. 'So thank you very much.'

'But not cheap enough for you to be able to stay open?' Allie asked.

'I'm afraid not. But I'm really thankful for all you've been doing. If we were staying open, I'd probably give you a pay rise, or promote you or something.'

'What would you promote me to?' asked Allie, interested.

'Chef in Charge of Home-made Food? Something like that?'

Allie smiled. 'I'd like that. Shame it's not going to happen.'

'Something good will happen for you, Allie. Your great attitude, your hard work, and the fact you're really good at baking, will all help you to get on.' He patted her on the shoulder. 'Hiring you was one of the best things I did. I acted on my gut feeling, and it turned out really well.'

Allie blushed. 'Thank you,' she managed to say before heading off to the stockroom. They were working out how they could use up all the stores before they closed.

A few mornings later, Allie opened up the café with Si. A week earlier she had decided to put fairy lights along the front of the building. The café would be closed well before Christmas, but the lights still looked pretty as the days got shorter.

She had already switched on the oven for the croissants and French sticks that Mac would be bringing in shortly. Now she was turning on the coffee machine and the fairy lights, and was making sure Jango's looked as warm and welcoming as it could. She could hear Mac and Si talking in the kitchen as she moved around, adjusting tables and chairs.

She had just unlocked the café door and turned the sign to 'Open' when there was a crash followed by a lot of swearing. She ran into the kitchen and saw Si on the floor, blood pouring from his hand. There was broken glass scattered around him.

'OK, Si,' said Mac calmly. 'Let's get you up. Can you bring a chair in, Allie?'

When Allie got back with the chair, Si was on his feet. His hand wrapped in a tea towel that was already soaked in blood.

'Sit down. Hold your arm up above your heart. I'm ringing the local hospital to tell them we're on our way. Allie? I think he needs another tea towel.'

Allie breathed deeply and tried not to panic. 'What happened?' she asked Si.

'I tripped on the step while I was bringing in the soft drinks, and landed on one of the bottles I dropped.'

'Oh. That's bad!'

Over the next few minutes, she did what Mac asked her to do, and smiled at Si when he made jokes about making a mess on the floor.

'It's OK. I'm used to clearing up after you in the kitchen,' she said.

'Right,' said Mac, having made his phone call. 'Allie, you ring Jessie and see if she's free and could come in and help you. If she can't – and she does have other work now – you could close up. You won't be able to manage on your own.' He smiled at her. 'Don't worry! I'll be back and we'll just open a bit late, that's all.'

The two men left and Allie went out to turn the sign to 'Closed', although she didn't want to.

She wanted Jango's to be open every minute it had left before it was closed for ever. There was a man sitting at a table, obviously expecting to be served. Then she remembered that she hadn't put up the sign asking people to ring the bell if there was no one behind the counter. Early in the morning, when everyone was in the kitchen cooking, customers needed to say they were there.

'I'm sorry! I didn't see you at first,' she said. 'What can I get you?' She could have explained that the café had to close, but didn't. It seemed wrong to send a customer away.

'Coffee and a croissant, please.'

Allie hesitated. 'I'm afraid we have no croissants. They haven't been collected from the bakery yet.'

'Hmm. So what about one of Allie's Cheese Scones?'

'I'm Allie and I haven't had a chance to make them. They take about thirty minutes if you'd like to wait?'

The man shook his head. He didn't seem very impressed.

'Toast?' said Allie.

The man shook his head. 'I could make toast at home. I've come out for breakfast. I want something a bit special. What have you got?'

Allie took a breath. She had to be brave. 'American pancakes with blueberry compote. We can offer you some cream with that. Maple syrup if you'd like.'

The man grinned. 'Now you're talking!'

'I haven't made the batter yet,' said Allie. 'But I'll get your coffee now, to keep you going.'

Allie had never made pancakes in the café before. She hadn't suggested them, because they'd had lots of things on offer for breakfast when they'd been collecting pastries from the bakery. But now she was checking the recipe in her notebook, which went with her everywhere, and she realised what a good idea they were. Much cheaper than bought-in products like croissants and Danish pastries.

She knew there was some blueberry compote in the fridge, because she'd taken it out of the freezer the day before, while trying to clear it out. There was cream too. Mac liked it with his fruit scone sometimes, instead of butter.

She sieved flour into a bowl, added baking powder and then an egg. She had whisked in the milk and sugar before she rushed out to refill the man's coffee.

At last she was able to bring through a plate with four pancakes, the compote in a little dish on the side, along with the cream.

'Now,' she said, 'I can't remember if you wanted maple syrup with that?'

'Yes please,' said the man, who was looking at his plate intently. Then he got out his phone.

'Are you going to put a picture on social media?' asked Allie.

'I think so. This plate is definitely good enough.'

Allie opened her mouth to say there was no point, the café was closing, but didn't. Jango's could close with everyone saying how good it was, having come to eat American pancakes for breakfast.

There were a couple more sets of customers by the time Mac and Si got back from A & E.

'Oh, you're back quickly! I thought you'd have to wait for ages to be seen,' she said.

Mac smiled. 'It wasn't crowded and Si was bleeding on to the floor. They took him in more or less straight away.'

'And I have a very big bandage and a sling to prove it,' said Si, holding up his hand.

'Well, that's good! But I have customers. I didn't turn the sign in time.' Allie smiled. 'I'd better see how they're getting on. I have a new addition to the menu I need to tell you about as well.'

Two other tables were having pancakes, as Allie had felt, once she'd made the batter, she might as well use it up. Then, of course, she'd run out of batter and had to make more.

The first man to order pancakes was still there, writing in a notebook. She was a bit surprised to see him as he'd paid earlier.

'Is the boss in?' he asked. 'It's after nine, now.'

'Yes, he is,' said Allie. 'He had to take a member of staff to A & E, which is why he wasn't here earlier.' Allie didn't want this stranger to think that Mac didn't turn up early to work.

'Would you mind asking him if I could have a word?' The man smiled, as if he knew he was being a bit cheeky.

Allie nodded and went into the kitchen. 'Mac? There's a man out there who wants to see you. And he had the American pancakes with blueberry compote and cream.'

'What?' Mac looked very surprised.

'We had no croissants and he didn't want toast. I had to improvise.'

Mac laughed. 'Turn my back for five minutes and you've put something new on the menu. Again!'

'It's a damn shame Jango's is closing,' said Si, sitting on a chair, slightly in the way.

'It's a shame you can't do anything useful with only one hand!' said Allie, tossing her head and laughing, as she opened the dishwasher and started to put cups in it.

'Actually, I could do that,' said Si, returning her smile. 'Fill the dishwasher, I mean.'

'Oh, thank you! Although I expect Mac will want to close up in a minute. If he's chatting, he's not working. So it's just me doing everything!' Although she was keeping up a cheerful front, Allie felt cross. She hated to be beaten. She wanted to work miracles in the café.

'You can do it, Allie! You're amazing!' said Si.

'Thank you! I do my best.' Allie switched on the dishwasher. She should have been thrilled that Si had said that. But instead, she just felt terribly sad that all this was coming to an end, although everyone had worked so hard to prevent it.

All morning Allie rushed about from serving to the kitchen and back again, making cappuccinos and flat whites and other sorts of coffee. Mac was still talking to the man. When he saw Allie looking stressed, he said, 'Actually, we're going to take this conversation to my flat. It's getting complex. Close up if you want to. You'll never cope without help.'

Allie smiled. In her head she told him that she'd managed this long, so she'd go on managing. She wasn't going to close Jango's unless she really had to.

She turned to her customers. She was getting them coffees, scones, whatever they wanted, but the tables were filling with dirty dishes. She loaded her tray with them and went back to the kitchen.

Si was mixing scone dough with one hand.

'Si! You should rest! You shouldn't be doing that!'

'While you're working flat out, I'm not going to let you or Jango's down.'

He grinned at her and suddenly she felt happy.

'We've got this!'

'We have!' He gave her a thumbs up with his good hand, covered in flour.

She went back out into the café to see Jock, a tray in his hand, clearing tables.

'Jock!'

'I could see you were busy, lass,' said Jock. 'I thought I'd lend a hand.'

'Thank you so much! If you take them through to Si, he's loading the dishwasher one-handed, when he's not making scones.'

By the time Allie got back to the kitchen, she found the dishwasher going and a batch of scones in the oven.

'Put the two of us together,' said Jock, now wearing an apron and a pair of chef's trousers, 'and you get a whole member of staff! And don't worry, I gave my hands a very good wash.'

'He knows his way round a kitchen,' said Si, obviously impressed

Jock nodded. 'I was in the catering trade, working in restaurants and bars, before I came down to London. Then I moved here.' He paused. 'Hard to get a job when you haven't got an address.'

'Thank you so much for helping out,' said Allie.

'You and Mac have helped me and my pal out often enough, with food and drink from this café. I'm happy to help out now.'

Mac came back late in the afternoon when Allie was turning the sign on the door to 'Closed'. She was so tired, even that small action seemed to take an effort.

'Hey! You guys!' said Mac. 'Don't tell me you've managed all this time with just the two of you?'

'It wasn't just us in the end,' said Allie.

'Oh? Did Jessie come in?'

Allie shook her head. 'No. Si can do quite a lot with only one hand and Jock helped.'

'Jock did?' Mac frowned. 'What did he do?'

'A lot! He's a trained chef! He helped Si make scones and sandwiches, things like that. He used to work in restaurants when he was still in Scotland.'

Mac looked thoughtful. 'Did he now? That's interesting.' Then he frowned. 'Are you dead on your feet or could we have a chat? You and Si – Jock too.'

'I'll make drinks,' said Allie, all her tiredness melting away. 'Your usual Americano with warm milk?'

Mac grinned. 'You're the best, Allie!'

Allie thought she heard Si say, 'She is,' but she wasn't quite sure. It made her heart give a little skip.

Chapter Twelve

When Mac, Allie, Si and Jock were all sitting round the table with hot drinks, Mac said, 'I expect you were wondering why I was wasting time talking to that guy – the one who so loved your pancakes, Allie – instead of helping out. Well, I've got news.'

'Looking at your face, it's good news,' said Jock.

'I think it is! Mr Lincoln has money to invest, and he wants to invest it in his home town, which is here.'

'And?' said Si. Mac had paused to take a sip of coffee.

'And he wants to buy the lease of the café. Even better – he wants to buy next door too. And I want to turn that place into a diner – somewhere people can eat in the evenings.'

'So Jango's won't close?' asked Allie.

'It will close, but just for a few weeks, to refurbish and knock through to next door,' said Mac. 'Your wages will be paid, so you'll stay with us and not go off and find a better job.'

'I would never do that!' said Allie. 'I love this café!'

Mac nodded. 'Mr Lincoln already knew Jango's had a good reputation in town and he saw how much you loved it, how you went the extra mile. It made him think it was a business worth investing in. So thank you for that.'

Allie blushed and played with her coffee.

'There'll be jobs going,' said Mac to Jock. 'If you were interested?'

'I'd be interested all right,' said Jock. 'Being homeless makes it difficult to find work.'

'Mr Lincoln wants to turn the space above next door into three flats. If you wanted to work for me, and I put a word in for you, maybe you could rent one of them?'

'Wow,' said Jock. His grin was so wide it seemed to split his face in two. 'That would be great.'

'I'm not sure how much work needs doing to make them ready for living in,' said Mac. 'But I hope not too much!'

'Pete – he's my mate – was in the building trade before his boss went bust,' said Jock. 'And we both know other guys who need work, so let us know if you need any demolition work, decorating, anything like that. We can probably find someone with the right skills.'

'I'll see what I can do.' Mac turned to Allie and Si. 'Well, you've worked hard today. Time I got you home. I'll give you both a lift. No driving for a while for you, Si, although I'll arrange to get your car home for you.'

Allie was grateful to relax into the front seat.

About ten minutes later they reached the end of Allie's road. 'OK, Allie. I'll put you down here. Si? Where do you live, exactly? I'll take you all the way home.'

'I'll get out here, if it's all the same to you,' he said to Mac. 'And OK with you, Allie?'

'Fine with me,' said Allie, trying not to show how delighted this made her. 'But what will you do afterwards? How will you get home?'

'Don't worry about me,' said Si. 'I don't live far away.'

Now they were away from the café, where they knew how to treat each other, walking down the road to her house felt a bit odd.

'Let's see if Cherry's in,' said Allie as they reached her neighbour's house. Cherry was relaxed with everyone, and she'd like to meet Si. There was a good chance her dad would be there, too.

Allie was right. 'Your dad's here,' said Cherry when she opened the door, obviously pleased to see them.

'Wow, Si! How did you get a bandage that big?' Derek said when they were sitting in the kitchen with mugs of tea.

Si told the story, but then said, 'But that's not the most interesting thing that happened today. Allie was a star!'

'Not surprised about that,' said Cherry.

'Tell us!' said Derek, looking at his daughter proudly.

'Well, do you remember teaching me to make American pancakes?' said Allie.

'Of course,' said Cherry.

'When a customer wanted croissants and we didn't have any because Mac had taken Si to A & E, I offered him toast. He was not impressed! He said he could have toast at home. So I remembered the pancakes. I knew we had blueberry compote in the fridge – we've been trying to empty the freezers and use up the stuff. Anyway, he loved them!'

Si took up the tale, about how Mac came back and got talking to Mr Lincoln. And how he and Allie thought they would never stop talking.

'But then,' Allie said, 'he asked us to join him and told us what they talked about.' She told them everything. 'So, there's going to be a diner next to the café, and more jobs for everyone,' Allie went on. 'And maybe Jock – remember?

The Scottish guy who saved me from Ryan with his friend?'

'Of course,' said Cherry. 'It's so good that he's going to benefit from all this. He's always so pleasant when you pass him.'

'I hope he will,' said Allie.

'I'm sure he will. He was great in the kitchen,' said Si as he stood up. 'I'd better get going. My hand is beginning to throb a bit.'

'You need to take another painkiller,' said Allie. 'Shall I get you some water?'

'That would be kind,' said Si.

'I'll run you home, lad,' said Derek when Si had taken his tablet. 'You look all in. You and Allie have had quite a day of it.'

'That's very kind of you,' said Si. 'I won't say no. I am a bit tired.' Then he looked at Allie in a way that told her he wanted to speak to her.

'Give us a minute, Dad,' said Allie. 'Si? I'll come out with you.'

'I've got to go home for my car keys,' said Derek. 'Meet you outside, Si?'

When they were on the doorstep, waiting for Derek to come back with the car keys, Si said, 'So!' He suddenly seemed a bit awkward although they'd been through so much together. He cleared his throat. 'Would you go out with me, Al?'

'What, now?' said Allie. 'I thought your hand was hurting!'

'I didn't mean now, this minute. I meant – you know – would you go out with me?'

It took Allie a minute to realise what Si was saying. 'You mean, like as if I was your girlfriend?'

'I've liked you for ages but I had a girlfriend. Our relationship was fading away, but until one of us finished it I couldn't say anything to you.'

Allie smiled. 'I get that.'

'So we could go and see a film or something? Or even go out for something to eat, so someone cooks for us?'

She and her dad had been out for pizza a couple of times, but Ryan had never taken her out for a meal. It would be really lovely.

'Can I have your number?' Si asked.

She took his phone and put in her number, and then he called her to check it. 'Right, we're sorted now. I'll call you tomorrow, if that's OK?'

She nodded again. She didn't want to speak in case her voice showed how thrilled she was.

Chapter Thirteen

Allie planned to go to her house to have a shower, but instead went back in to thank Cherry for tea and help her clear up the mugs.

As she stacked the dishwasher, Cherry said, 'I think your dad wants a word with you when he comes back from dropping off Si.'

'Oh? Is it about you two?' Allie sounded bright and enthusiastic. 'I'm so happy for you.'

'I'm glad you feel like that, but Derek still needs to talk to you. Not about that.'

Allie went home and had a shower, wondering what her dad could want to talk about that she didn't already know. But she was so excited about Si asking her out, she wasn't going to spoil that lovely feeling by thinking about it too much.

She was downstairs drying her hair with a towel when he came back in.

'Hi, love,' said Derek. 'Mind if I have a lager? Want one?'

'No, thanks.' She was getting nervous now. Her dad was being a bit weird.

He sat on the sofa with his can. 'That's a nice lad you've got there,' he said.

'Si? Yes, he is nice. He's a hard worker, too.'

Although neither of them said anything, they both knew they were thinking about Ryan. No one would ever have said he was a hard worker.

'So ...' Derek played with the can in his hands, looking very uncomfortable.

Allie decided to help him out. 'Dad, it's OK. I know about you and Cherry getting together. I'm very happy about it!'

'I'm really glad, but haven't you worried about the house, where you're going to live? Cherry and myself want to move in together. She's just renting next door. If it works out, we'll buy somewhere together.'

Suddenly Allie understood that what she had dreaded was really happening.

'But you could go on living here.' Derek took a sip of his lager. Allie could tell he was thinking about how to go on.

'OK ...' Allie said slowly.

'You know your mum didn't want to leave you. It broke her heart when you came back here to me.'

Allie was surprised. What did her mother have to do with it? But she nodded. 'I know, Dad. I never felt she left me. She didn't come home and I would have liked that, but she was always my mum. I knew she loved me – loves me! It's not like she's dead.'

Derek chuckled. 'No. She may live in Canada, but she's good about keeping in touch.'

Allie nodded. 'I know. And you used to send her photos of me, along with the crazy cards I used to make.'

She was smiling, but remembered how thrilled her mother had always been to get them, even though Allie was sure all the bits of sparkle she'd stuck on had probably fallen off in the envelope. She'd been teased at school for not having a mum, but *she'd* never felt she didn't have a mum. Her mum just lived in another country.

'Well, she did another thing for you that you didn't know about,' said Derek.

'What's that?'

'You know your mum's band had one hit?'

Allie giggled. 'It wasn't a big hit, but it was hers. I loved it when I was little. I was so happy when it was the music for that shampoo ad. Every time it came on telly I was so excited!'

'You were so proud of your mum.'

'I was.'

'Well, before she left for Canada with your stepfather—'

'I don't think of him as a stepfather,' said Allie.

'Well, whatever,' said Derek. 'Before she left she made over the rights to that song to you. That was before the advert, but she was thrilled when she knew it was going to earn much more money.'

Allie was confused. 'What are you saying, Dad?'

'I'm saying that, over the years, payments have been coming in for you from that song. I've been looking after the money, and your mum and I agreed I should use it to pay off the mortgage. This house is now yours. I've put it in your name.'

Allie rubbed her forehead, hoping it would help her understand what her dad had just said. 'The house is mine?'

'Yes. I didn't tell you about it when you were going out with Ryan. If he'd known you owned a house, even a small one, he would never have let you go.'

'I let *him* go, Dad!'

'But he would have made life even more difficult for you. He might even have married you before you worked out what a loser he was,' Derek said.

'You never said anything about him when we were together,' said Allie.

'It wouldn't have helped, love. Trust me.'

'So now you're saying that, thanks to Mum, I own this house?'

'And there's a bit in an account I thought you could use to go and visit her, when the time was right.'

'I don't know what to say, Dad!' Allie was stunned.

'I'll make you a cup of tea. We'll talk it through until you're clear about it.'

Allie sipped tea and they talked about her owning the house and then she had a thought. 'But, Dad, if you and Cherry want to buy a house together, if it works out between you, what will you use for money? If I own this house?'

'You're very caring but you needn't worry. I put all the money I would have spent on the mortgage into another house, which I've been renting out. I can sell that and use it to buy a house with Cherry.'

'I don't know what to say, Dad! It's all a bit of a shock.'

He crunched his lager can with his hands. 'I should have told you sooner, but you know how it is. I didn't tell you in the beginning because you were too young to understand, and then it was never the right moment. And then you got together with Ryan – and you were very young when that happened.'

He paused. 'But it seems the right time to tell you now.' He patted her knee awkwardly. 'I'm so proud of you. You've got a job that you love because you learned new things. Your mum will be so proud of you too.'

Allie felt a bit choked up. She cleared her throat. 'I'll ring her later and tell her about the job and everything. And that now might be a good time to visit, because Jango's is going to be closed for a bit. What a day! It started with me going to work thinking the café was going to close, and it's ended with me having a new boy-friend, a steady job and a house!' She smiled at her dad and rubbed his arm. 'A lot of it's down to Cherry. She taught me to cook.'

'You rescued her wheelie bin. She hasn't forgotten.'

'Anyone would have done that!' said Allie, laughing.

But Derek shook his head. 'But *you* did it. You learned to cook and got your dream job. And it's partly down to you the café was saved. You saved the day, Allie!'

Allie went in for a hug. 'Oh, Dad!'

The Recipes

Katie Fforde's Chocolate Brownies

Makes 15 brownies

100 g nuts (a selection of macadamia, Brazil, pecan and hazelnuts, but hazelnuts on their own work well)
50 g dark chocolate (at least 75% cocoa solids)
110 g butter
2 large eggs, beaten
225 g caster sugar
50 g flour, plain or self-raising
1 level tsp baking powder
¼ tsp salt
1 tsp vanilla extract

Prepare a 18 × 28 cm tray lined with baking parchment. The paper should come about 2.5 cm above the edges of the tin. If you haven't a tray this exact size you can use a smaller or bigger tin, but remember the cooking time won't be the same. Cook for a shorter time if the tin is larger, as the mixture will be more spread out and thinner. A smaller tin will take a bit longer.

Chop the nuts roughly. You could put them in a plastic bag and hit them with a rolling pin. You don't want them too small. Then toast them carefully in an oven for 8 minutes, or you can put them in a dry frying pan and toast them that way.

Put the chocolate and the butter in a bowl and put it over a bowl of boiling water. Stir until melted. Or you could melt the butter in the microwave first and add it to the chocolate. (Cold butter takes ages to melt for some reason.)

When the chocolate and butter are melted add all the other ingredients and stir well.

Spread the mixture into the tin and cook for about 30 minutes until slightly springy in the centre. Leave to cool for 10 minutes or so before cutting into small squares. Then put the squares on to a wire rack to cool.

Katie's Tip

I always double this recipe as people eat them so quickly!

Nick Nairn's Cheese Scones

Makes 8 scones

230 g plain flour
3 tsp baking powder
½ tsp salt
A pinch of cayenne
55 g butter, plus extra for serving
125 g grated cheese, plus extra for topping
150 ml milk
150 ml water
1 egg (for eggwash)
Preheat the oven to 210 °C, or gas mark 8.

Sift the dry ingredients into a big bowl. Rub in the butter and then fold in the grated cheese (I use ⅔ Cheddar, ⅓ Parmesan). Add all the milk and mix with a fork. Then add the water in three 50 ml measures until the mix is thick and sticky.

Use a bit of flour on your hands and board, and pat out the mixture to 2 cm thick, then cut into 8 squares (I use a dough scraper but a knife is OK). Put on to a buttered baking sheet. Add a bit of eggwash and a little more grated cheese on top.

Bake for 15 to 20 minutes until nicely coloured. Cool on a rack for another 20 minutes, and then go for it with extra butter!

Nick's Tip

Cutting the scones with a knife and not a cutter means you don't have to re-roll the mixture which means it's all lighter.

Louisa Carter's Fluffy American Pancakes

This easy American pancake recipe makes light and fluffy pancakes that are great for a weekend brunch. Try adding a large handful of fresh blueberries to the batter before cooking.

Serves 4

135 g plain flour
1 tsp baking powder
½ tsp salt
2 tbsp caster sugar (or less, according to taste)
130 ml milk
1 large egg, lightly beaten
2 tbsp melted butter (allowed to cool slightly) or olive oil, plus extra for cooking maple syrup and more butter to serve

Sift the flour, baking powder, salt and caster sugar into a large bowl. In a separate bowl or jug, lightly whisk together the milk and egg, then whisk in the melted butter.

Pour the milk mixture into the flour mixture and, using a fork, beat until you have a smooth batter. Any lumps will soon disappear with a little mixing. Let the batter stand for a few minutes.

Heat a non-stick frying pan over a medium heat and add a knob of butter. When it's melted, add a ladle of batter (or two if your frying pan is big enough to cook two pancakes at the same time). It will seem very thick but this is how it should be. Wait until the top of the pancake begins to bubble, then turn it over and cook until both sides are golden brown and the pancake has risen to about 1 cm thick.

Repeat until all the batter is used up. You can keep the pancakes warm in a low oven, but they taste best fresh out of the pan.

Serve with lashings of real maple syrup and extra butter, if you like.

Louisa's Tips

For extra-fluffy pancakes, substitute self-raising flour for plain flour and still use the baking powder. Serve the pancakes with fresh strawberries and good vanilla ice cream.

You can also use half buckwheat flour and half plain flour and serve with maple syrup and bacon. You can also add 1 tsp ground cinnamon to the buckwheat batter and serve with caramelised apple slices and thick double cream.

THE READING AGENCY

About Quick Reads

"Reading is such an important building block for success"
- Jojo Moyes

Quick Reads are short books written by best-selling authors. They are perfect for regular readers and those who are still to discover the pleasure of reading.

Did you enjoy this Quick Read?
Tell us what you thought by filling in our short survey. Scan the QR code to go directly to the survey or visit
https://bit.ly/QuickReads2021

Turn over to find your next Quick Read…

A special thank you to Jojo Moyes for her generous donation and support of Quick Reads and to Here Design.

Quick Reads is part of The Reading Agency, a national charity tackling life's big challenges through the proven power of reading.

www.readingagency.org.uk
@readingagency   #QuickReads

The Reading Agency Ltd. Registered number: 3904882 (England & Wales)
Registered charity number: 1085443 (England & Wales)
Registered Office: Free Word Centre, 60 Farringdon Road, London, EC1R 3GA
The Reading Agency is supported using public funding by Arts Council England.

Supported using public funding by
**ARTS COUNCIL
ENGLAND**

Find your next Quick Read:
the 2021 series

Available to buy in paperback or ebook and
to borrow from your local library.

More from Quick Reads

For a complete list of titles and more information on the authors and their books visit

www.readingagency.org.uk/quickreads

Continue your reading journey

The Reading Agency is here to help keep you
and your family reading:

Challenge yourself to complete six reads
by taking part in Reading Ahead
at your local library, college or workplace
readingahead.org.uk

Join Reading Groups for Everyone to find a
reading group and discover new books
readinggroups.org.uk

Celebrate reading on World Book Night
every year on 23 April
worldbooknight.org

Read with your family as part of the
Summer Reading Challenge
at your local library
summerreadingchallenge.org.uk

For more information, please visit our website:
readingagency.org.uk

Have you read them all?

Living Dangerously
For Polly, life is complicated enough without a relationship. Surely, love is only a distraction...

The Rose Revived
May, Sally and Harriet decide to kick-start their own business. Is it too much to hope for the same in their romantic lives?

Wild Designs
When Althea loses her job, she decides to transform her life and pursue her passion for gardening.

Stately Pursuits
Hetty is drawn into a fight to save a crumbling stately home.

Life Skills
When Julia goes to work on a pair of hotel boats, her past follows her...

Thyme Out
Perdita runs into her ex-husband unexpectedly. Can love blossom between them for a second time?

Artistic Licence
Thea runs off to Ireland with a charming artist and finds herself having to choose between two men.

Highland Fling
Jenny Porter dashes off to Scotland and gets caught in a complicated love triangle...

Paradise Fields
Which man can Nel trust to help preserve the meadow and farmers' market she loves?

Restoring Grace
Ellie and Grace embark on restoring a stately home, but have to reckon with the help of the disconcertingly attractive Flynn Cormack.

Flora's Lot
Flora joins the family antique business and finds herself fending off dinner invitations from the devastatingly handsome Henry.

Practically Perfect
Anna decides to renovate a beautiful cottage that is perfect on the outside but anything but on the inside.

Going Dutch
Jo and Dora live on a barge boat and have both sworn off men until they meet Marcus and Tom...

Wedding Season
Complications ensue when wedding planner Sarah agrees to plan two weddings on the same day.

Love Letters

When the bookshop where she works has to close, Laura agrees to help organise a literary festival, with complicated results...

A Perfect Proposal

Fed up with living her life for others, Sophie jets off to New York for the trip of a lifetime.

Summer of Love

Sian moves to the country with her young son to start a new life.

Recipe for Love

Zoe is invited to compete in a televised cookery competition. There is only one problem; one of the judges is too tasty to resist...

A French Affair

When Gina inherits a stall in the French House and meets the owner, the last thing she is thinking about is love...

The Perfect Match

Bella is dismayed when the man who broke her heart, many years ago, turns up in her life again.

A Vintage Wedding

Beth, Lindy and Rachel set up a business organising beautiful vintage weddings. Could their own happy endings be right around the corner?

A Summer at Sea
Emily decides to spend the summer cooking on a
'puffer' boat in Scotland.

A Secret Garden
Lorna and Philly work at a beautiful manor house
in the Cotswolds. Could everything change when
they discover a secret garden?

A Country Escape
Fran has a year to turn a very run-down dairy farm
into profit. What could possibly go wrong?

A Rose Petal Summer
Will this be the summer Caro and the young man
she met in Greece many years previously finally
fall in love?

A Springtime Affair
Gilly falls for the charming Leo, while her
daughter Helena accepts a helping hand from Jago.
Can both these men be too good to be true?

Keep in touch with

Katie Fforde

Step into the world of Katie Fforde at

www.katiefforde.com

**Be the first to hear Katie's news by
signing up to her email newsletter,
find out all about her new book releases
and see Katie's photos and videos.**

You can also follow Katie on twitter
or visit her dedicated Facebook page

 @KatieFforde

 /katiefforde